Owen Innsly

Love Poems and Sonnets

Owen Innsly

Love Poems and Sonnets

ISBN/EAN: 9783744771252

Printed in Europe, USA, Canada, Australia, Japan

Cover: Foto ©Andreas Hilbeck / pixelio.de

More available books at **www.hansebooks.com**

Love

Poems and Sonnets

BY

OWEN INNSLY

BOSTON

CUPPLES, UPHAM & COMPANY

OLD CORNER BOOKSTORE

1883

Third Edition.

PRESS OF
STANLEY AND USHER,
BOSTON, MASS.

DEDICATION.

Mov'st thou, perchance, in strange and
    starry spheres
Afar, beyond the impenetrable night
That shrouds the tomb, smiling at the
    old fears
Of death, encircled by all-conquering
    light?
Or dost thou sleep where thy last bed
    was made,
Beneath the violets and the scented
    grass,
Careless alike of sunshine and of shade,
Of morns that linger and of eves that
    pass?

Ah! who shall say? No eye can pierce
    the dark,
No strained ear tidings catch of weal or
    woe
Out of the silence; and no single spark
Illumes that portal through which all
    must go.

Yet this we know : Death is a kind of
     birth,
And brings one sacred immortality ;
Thou livest in thy traces left on earth ;
Thou livest in thy children's memory.

And one of these, binding the varied
     flowers,
With tinted petals and with shining
     leaves,
Fall'n on his path in sad and happy
     hours,
As one might bind the ripened corn in
     sheaves,
Dear blossoms of the heart and brain, —
     such sprays
And blooms as wither not, but nod and
     wave
Forever, — the completed garland lays
With loving hands upon thy quiet grave.

CONTENTS.

	PAGE
Dedication	7

LOVE POEMS AND SONNETS.

Waiting	15
Nature and Love	17
Helen	20
An Evening Ride	24
Departure	26
Cui Bono?	28
A Dream of Death	30
The Better Part	33
Compensation	35
Gifts of the Gods	37
Shadows	39
A Rosary	40
Helena's Song	41
Amor Leggero	42
Burnt Ships	44
Outre-Mort	45
Light-Houses	47
Laurels	49

	PAGE
Jewels	51
Liebesbitte	53
My Queen	54
" One Way of Love "	56
Mortalis	58
Thine Eyes	60
Dependence	62
Submission	64
Love's Calendar	65
Islands	67
Snow-Drops	69
Love's Abode	71
Storm and Calm	73
Serving	75
The Burden of Love	77
A Simile	78
Blossoms of Love	79
Deprecation	81
Nepenthe	83
Σὺ Σωτήρ	84
In a Letter	86
Titles	88
After Absence	90
Bondage	92
Witch-Hazel	93
Calm	95
Symphonie Fantastique	97
Idem non Aliter	98

PAGE

The Sleeping Beauty 99
Friendship and Love 102
The Troubadour 104
"The Greek Youth" 106
Wanderleben 108
Her Roses 110
At the Convent 112
Faust and Helena 113
Two Figures 116
Service 118
Communion 120

MISCELLANEOUS.

Impatience 125
Im Freien 127
Propitiation 129
Musa Loquitur 131
Waking 133
The Rose and the Statue 136
Wonders 138
In Memoriam 141
From Naples to Rome 144
Giardino Giusti 146
Fountains in Rome 148
A Roma 150
On the Pincian 152
Aftermath 155
A Prayer 157

PAGE

Χαῖρε | 158

Schumann's Symphony in B Flat
    Major 160

Joachim 162

Rubinstein 163

Chopin 165

"Mein Tag war heiter, glücklich
    meine Nacht" 167

To R. W. E. 169

Chaucer 171

At Sea 173

A Voyage 176

Kings 178

Weaving 180

A Shattered Glass 182

Surplus 184

Florence 186

Shelley 188

Cor Cordium 189

Rome after 1870 191

To Rome 193

Antinous of the Vatican 197

A Bas-Relief 199

Addio a Roma 201

On Leaving Italy 202

LOVE POEMS AND SON-NETS.

WAITING.

I COUNT the days, —
The lovely days, the weary days ;
From east to west they softly go,
    Silent and slow.

Green is the earth
With budding grass ; the wondrous birth
Of spring and hope, wide as it spreads,
    New glory sheds.

The air is sweet.
Here snowy petals strew the street ;
Here lean against the garden-wall
    The lilacs tall.

The cuckoo cries,
And in his frequent note there lies

The count of years where brain and
    nerve
      Must toil and serve.[1]

      But youth is strong,
And unappalled it fronts the long
Array of days — which must be fair
      If thou art there —

      When I may learn
My will to thine to bend and turn,
To meet thy mood, and more and more
      Love and adore.

      The world is dear
And good; I dare not shed a tear.
I sing my songs of love and praise,
      And count the days.

DRESDEN, *May,* 1875.

---

[1] There is a German superstition that one who
listens to the cuckoo will live as many years as he
hears repetitions of the bird's cry.

NATURE AND LOVE.

Day after day I watch the fine
       Dividing line,
Scarcely discerned, 'twixt sea and sky;
       Beneath me lie
Smooth shining sands, and overhead
       Clear heavens outspread.

Day after day, through balmy hours,
       I pluck the flowers
From heavy-laden shrub and tree;
       The fleur-de-lis,
Purple and tall, and blue-eyed grass
       Bloom where I pass.

Often the wood-bird's clear note rings,
       And insect wings
Flit gay and glittering down the breeze;
       And gold-ringed bees
Drink from a fragrant flower-cup
       Its sweet draughts up.

Here 'mid the scented pines I dream,
    Until I seem
A monarch in an ancient time,—
    A time sublime,
When earth gave all men, frank and free,
    What she gives me.

But often, when the restless waves
    My light boat braves,
A mariner destined to explore
    An unknown shore
Am I.   All day beneath the sun,
    My voyage begun,

I sing glad songs of conquering men,
    Though silent when
The moon her pale flame lights above,
    And crowned with love.
What in that word I half express,
    Dost thou not guess ?

A dearer hope than nature gives
    Forever lives,
Filling my soul.   There floods my heart
    A joy apart
From seas or flowers or glowing noons,
    Or suns or moons.

Through all the glory and the grace
    I see thy face ;
In the waves' whisper, soft and clear,
    Thy voice I hear ;
Thy smile through every hour doth fall,
    And blesses all.

HELEN.

WITHOUT the walls of Troy the Grecian
host,
Encamped, lay, spent and weary with the
fight.
Eve after eve they watched the golden
light
Of suns whose splendors seemed to
mock them most
When most they prayed ; for morn on
morn they rose
To suffer fresh defeats and bear new
woes.

They could not curse, because she was
so fair,
The cause of all the ruin ; but the bands
Of heroes stretched to heaven beseech-
ing hands,
While, wrung from lips grown pallid
with despair,

A cry arose throughout the camp's do-
    main,
Reëchoing far across the barren plain,
      Till all the midnight air
      One name did bear, —
      Helen ! Helen ! Helen !

Within the walls of Troy the fires blazed
    bright,
And song and dance were gay, and wine
    flowed free,
Where, flushed with joy and pride and
    victory,
They held their revels far into the night,
Nor paused to listen to the warning
    voice
That bade them rather tremble than re-
    joice.

But lifting high their wine-cups crowned
    with flowers,
" O loveliest lady of the land of Greece,
Whose bright eyes, bringing glory, lead
    to peace,
We drink to thee through all the happy
    hours,"

They cried, and poured the crimson
    juices out,
Pledging her deep and long with shout
    on shout,
      Till all the midnight air
        One name did bear, —
          Helen ! Helen ! Helen !

Our hearts are battle-fields ; within them
    rage
The conflicts that despair and doubt and
    pain
With love and beauty and their count-
    less train
Of pleasures and of pomps forever wage.
Now Sorrow spreads her pall and claims
    the fight ;
Now her pale hosts surrender to de-
    light.

But whether, tossing on mad waves of
    joy,
I drink great draughts of rapture as of
    wine,
Or, sunk beneath a chill and bitter
    brine,
I lie the prey of every vile annoy,

One image 'rules each smile, controls
    each sigh,
And like the men of old to her I cry,
    Till all the midnight air
      One name doth bear —
       Helen ! Helen ! Helen !

AN EVENING RIDE.

FROM GLASHÜTTE TO MÜGELN IN SAXONY.

WE ride and ride.   High on the hills
  The fir-trees stretch into the sky ;
The birches, which the deep calm stills
  Quiver again as we speed by.

Beside the road a shallow stream
  Goes leaping o'er its rocky bed :
Here lie the corn-fields with a gleam
  Of daisies white and poppies red.

A faint star trembles in the west ;
  A fire-fly sparkles, fluttering bright
Against the mountain's sombre breast ;
  And yonder shines a village light.

Oh ! could I creep into thine arms
  Beloved ! and upon thy face

Read the arrest of dire alarms
  That press me close; from thy em-
    brace

View the sweet earth as on we ride.
  Alas! how vain our longings are!
Already night is spreading wide
  Her sable wing, and thou art far.

DEPARTURE.

THE hours go on.
Up from the leaden-colored sea
The autumn wind sweeps chillingly,
And she is gone.

Like tears that drain
The heart until its springs are dry,
So drains the sources of the sky
The falling rain.

The white ships sail
Like ghosts towards some mysterious
    tryst
Hastening ; and vanish in the mist,
Silent and pale.

From clasping hands
And clinging lips, from love and care
Of dear ones left, they dear ones bear
To unknown lands.

The circling shore
Lies lonely; the receding wave
Moans like that whisper from the grave
Heard evermore

By widowed hearts:
" Unfettered by the bonds of years,
And deaf to prayers, untouched by tears,
Each one departs."

O Love! O Grief!
Your mingled notes I singing wake,
With trust that song for her dear sake
May bring relief.

CUI BONO?

WHEREFORE the vigils and the tears,
The flight of dreams when night appears,
The short repose, the long unrest,
The wearied throbbings of the breast,
And utter impotence of will;
The shifting of the pillow till
A dull beam strikes the window-pane
And daylight struggles in again?

Were it indeed for her dear sake —
If she might slumber while I wake —
If, for my tossings to and fro,
Her limbs profounder rest might know —
But sleep, because it shuns my eyes,
On hers no whit the gentler lies;
And all the tears that I can shed
Bring no new blessing to her bed.

O Love! how overbold art thou.
I am thy slave; my heart I bow.

But one grace I demand of thee :
Torture not unavailingly.
Let mercy guide thee ; do not keep
Chained in thy toils the swift-winged
     Sleep.
Give me, too ceaselessly oppressed,
A little while a little rest.

A DREAM OF DEATH.

HELENA.

Du hast mich beschworen aus dem Grab
  Durch deinen Zauberwillen,
Belebtest mich mit Wollustgluth,
  Jetzt kannst du die Gluth nicht stillen.

Press deinen Mund auf meinen Mund,
  Der Menschen Odem ist göttlich,
Ich trinke deine Seele aus,
  Die Todten sind unersättlich.
                              HEINE.

I died; they wrapped me in a shroud,
With hollow mourning, far too loud,
And sighs that were but empty sound,
And laid me low within the ground.
I felt *her* tears through all the rest;
Past sheet and shroud they reached my
        breast;

They warmed to life the frozen clay,
And I began to smile and say :
   At last thou lov'st me, Helena !

I rose up in the dead of night ;
I sought her window ; — 't was a-light.
A pebble clattered 'gainst the pane, —
" Who 's there ? the wind and falling
     rain ? "
" Ah ! no ; but one thy tears have led
To leave his chill and narrow bed
To warm himself before thy breath ;
Who for thy sake has conquered death.
   Arise, and love me, Helena ! "

She oped the door, she drew me in.
Her mouth was pale, her cheek was
     thin ;
Her eyes were dim ; its length unrolled,
Fell loosely down her hair of gold.
My presence wrought her grief's eclipse ;
She pressed her lips upon my lips,
She held me fast in her embrace,
Her hands went wandering o'er my face :
   At last thou lov'dst me, Helena !

The days are dark, the days are cold,
And heavy lies the churchyard mould.

But ever, at the deep of night,
Their faith the dead and living plight.
Who would not die if certain bliss
Could be foreknown ? and such as this
No life — away ! the hour is nigh,
With heart on fire she waits my cry :
   Arise, and love me, Helena !

THE BETTER PART.

BECAUSE in love, my love! there are
Two parts to choose, the near, the far,
The humble moth, the glittering star;

Since one is vassal, one is lord,
One the adorer, one the adored,
One speaks, and one obeys the word;

Since one must watch and ever keep
A faithful guard that one may sleep,
Since one must sow, and one must reap;

Since one must wear, and one adorn,
One pluck the rose, and one the thorn,
One know the night, and one the morn;

Since one must give, and one must take,
One yield his heart for one to break,
Content e'en thus for love's dear sake;

I, dearest, choose the better part;
I choose the sorrow and the smart,
The full surrender of the heart.

I choose the better part to-day,
Forever, which no fate can sway,
And nought but death can take away.

COMPENSATION.

SINCE Heaven has given to me to wear
The crown of love august and fair,
Is it not fit that I should bear
Its cross as well, without despair?

Since I may sow the precious seed,
And cull its flowers to fill my need,
Is it a fatal thing indeed
If from their thorns my hands must
    bleed?

Since I may drink the draught divine
Down to the dregs, if sometimes brine
Be mingled with the glowing wine,
Shall I then murmur or repine?

O thou! who — whatsoe'er thou art,
Thou great and universal heart!
Thou soul of love! since pain and smart
Form of thy perfect whole a part,

My destined portion let me take,
While at thy boundless streams I slake
My thirst and gather strength to make
A joy of sorrow for love's sake.

GIFTS OF THE GODS.

THE gods bestow on men wisdom and
    art
To stir with noble counsel and brave
    deed
The flagging pulses of a fellow-heart,
      And minister to need.

To pierce the subtle secrets of the
    globe ;
To read the records of the lands and
    seas :
And stars that seam the midnight's sa-
    ble robe —
      Great Nature's mysteries.

And that all lore the breasts of all may
    reach,
And into new exalted regions lift,
They send the power of soul-compelling
    speech,
      And song's diviner gift.

From me they veiled their higher knowl-
    edge, hid
The paths of light and ·calm that lie
    above
The common round — my feeble lisp-
    ings chid,
        But taught me how to love.

SHADOWS.

SHE leaned from out the mystic space
   Of Shadow-land.   As on the wall
The shapes the fire-light casts, her face
   Flickered and faded ; — that was all.

Like phantoms starting on the wold,
   When dusk defeats the clear-eyed day,
Her form rose ; but when arms would
      hold
   And clasp, it vanished quite away.

Now we are shadows both.   Above
   The grave of hoped-for, future bliss
Two pale wraiths stand. O Sister !
      Love !
   Reach me thy lips. Can shadows
      kiss ?

A ROSARY.

LIKE pearls that form a rosary,
  So lie in shining rows for me,
Strung on a golden thread of Time,
  The precious hours I know with thee.

And, filled with love and praise of thee,
  As one who tells his rosary,
I count upon the beads of Time
  The benisons thou bringest me.

Oh ! may such hours still dawn for me,
  So rich in love, so filled with thee,
And glisten on the robe of Time
  A never-ending rosary.

HELENA'S SONG.

BETWEEN the olives and the pines
   The vineyards slope to meet the shore.
The sun in skies unsullied shines
   Till evening lends a charm the more.

The fragrant breath of orange-flowers
   Perfumes the sleepy summer air,
And all the slow-revolving hours
   A garb of pomp and beauty wear.

What were it all, O Love! my Love!
   But that with thee its joy I know?
Thou art my dazzling heaven above,
   And thou my fertile field below.

Thou art my wave-encircled land,
   And thou alone my central sea.
My spirit leaps at thy demand
   To drown, to lose itself in thee.

AMOR LEGGERO.

CHE son io per te ?
Una rosa che il fiato
Del caso ti soffia sul sentier,
Destando nel cor tuo triste e scorag-
giato
Della sua primavera un breve pensier.
Raccogli per poco l' umil fior,
Ed egli si muor.

Che sei tu per me ?
Un dolce e caldo raggio
Che manda della vita il piu bel sol,
A ranimar nel petto i cari dì del Maggio,
Mentre il mondo intier del freddo si
duol.
Ma cade la notte e il mio cor
S'agghiaccia allor.

Ebben, e sia cosi !
Non pianger si picciol cosa.

Godiamo almen la fugace felicità.
Godiamo il caldo del sol, il soave odor
    della rosa,
Finchè la notte vien e il profumo sen
    va.
Coprimi di baci mentre l'amor
Vive ancor.

BURNT SHIPS.

See H. H.'s Sonnet, " Burnt Ships."

UPON the hopeless desert of her love
I landed, lured by glamours on her face.
And, scarce on shore, — a desolate
    strange place, —
I said, — but surely some green cedar
    grove
Awaits me, proffering its cooling shade,
And in its depths melodious fountains
    spring.
So tear the canvas from the masts and
    bring
Planks, beams, and spars until the pile
    be laid.
Then with my own mad hands I lit the
    fire,
And watched with fevered eyes the dark
    mass burn,
So blotting out the prospect of return.
But daily cools the pulse of my desire,
And bitter is the redness of her lips.
Oh! god of love, why did I burn my
    ships?

OUTRE-MORT.

SUPPOSE the dreaded messenger of
    death
Should hasten steps that seem, though
    sure, so slow,
And soon should whisper with his chilly
    breath :
"Arise ! thine hour has sounded, thou
    must go ;
For they that earliest taste life's holiest
    feast
Must early fast, lest, grown too bold,
    they dare
Of them that follow after seize the
    share."
Then, though my pulse's beat forever
    ceased,
If where I slumbered thou shouldst
    chance to pass,
Though grave-bound, I thy presence
    should discern.

Heedless of coffin-lid and tangled grass,
Upward to kiss thy feet my lips would
      yearn ;
And did one spark of love thy heart in-
      flame,
With the old rapture I should call thy
      name.

LIGHT-HOUSES.

WHEN pales the sunset flush along the
    sky,
When the sea's azure deepens into gray,
The light-house lamps flash out across
    the bay,
Their cheerful beams proclaiming, —
    " This way lie
Perils, and that way safety: ye who
    roam,
Searching for foreign shores, with cau-
    tion steer ;
And ye returning, lo ! the land is near,
And yonder waits the harbor which is
    home."
Such is thy part ; thou art my beacon-
    light
Standing the open passage to disclose,
Against unsafe and treacherous ways to
    warn.

Nor ever did a dark and stormy night
Obscure my path, but that bright flame
    arose
And shone with steadfast radiance till
    the morn.

.

LAURELS.

I WOULD cull laurels — not for pride or
    fame.
When grave shades fall on him that lieth
    low,
All honor shrivels to an empty name ;
Alike are praise and blame, sunshine
    and snow.
But I would pluck the rarest flowers that
    spring
From mortal effort, gems that deepest
    sleep
In human possibility, to fling
Low at thy feet the gorgeous glittering
    heap,
That endless splendors might thy name
    surround ;
That men beholding thine imperial mien,
And the rich jewels wherewith thou wert
    crowned,
Might cry with awed, rapt voice : " Be-
    hold the queen ! "

That thou, so greeted, might'st grow
    proud the while,
And know love's work and bless me with
    a smile.

JEWELS.

KINGS have a royal custom that I love.
In common times bringing the priceless
  gems
That on high fête-days crown their dia-
  dems,
And of each stone setting the name
  above,
As, — This is such a pearl; such dia-
  mond this ;
They spread them where the general eye
  may see
And grow to brilliance in their brilliancy.
I too have jewels, jewels of pure bliss,
Brighter than pearls and diamonds, and
  more rare, —
Of song, speech, silence, presence, ab-
  sence ; turn
Which way you will their deathless
  splendors burn ;

So by my mood men guess which one I
    wear,
And in my gladness see the others shine,
For I am faint with joy to know them
    mine.

LIEBESBITTE.

In years to come I ask thee not to say:
" I loved him once ; once I did hold him
          dear : "
Ah no ! long since I put that hope away,
And buried it in smiles, without a tear.
But say : " 'Mid all who worshipped at
          my feet,
Exalting me, 'mid all who loved me best,
As I remember now, I think there beat
No heart more fondly in a single breast,
No eyes that brightened quicker when I
          came,
No hand that lay more longingly in mine,
No voice that knew a tenderer tone to
          name
My name than his whose love seemed
          half divine."
If this thou say, though I be dead the
          while,
The words will reach me, I shall hear
          and smile.

MY QUEEN.

SHE has been queen too long whom I
  adore,
Mistress of men and moulder of their
  will,
For homage such as mine to reach the
  core
Of her proud heart, or teach it one new
  thrill.
Yet have I heard that royal rulers know
Such greed for power, that, for some strip
  of land,
Some province stored with vineyards, or
  where stand
Long rows of waving corn and grain,
  they throw,
Like rubbish, honor, wealth, and fame
  away,
And, as 't were water, spill the blood of
  men.
If this be so, perchance to increase thy
  sway

By one poor heart's extent thou 'rt fain.
 Oh! then
Stretch out thy hand to me, and with a
 mien
Of graciousness look on me, oh! my
 queen.

"ONE WAY OF LOVE."

To love thee, sweet, is as if one should
    love
A marble statue of perfected form,
Which, on the spot that hot lips lie
    above,
A tiny spot, grows for an instant warm :
The moment passed, straightway 't is
    cold again,
Returning to its first proud lifeless
    grace ;
Keeping no memory of the close em-
    brace.
Nor from the warm red lips one scarlet
    stain.
But what of that ? Why should I be
    distressed
Though thou art cold as stone ? Let me
    be brave
If but for once, and love for nothing
    save

For love's sake only; for he loveth best
And brightest does his flame of passion
    burn
Who giveth all things asking no return.

MORTALIS.

IF thou shouldst die, Belovèd, — fatal
    thought
That curdles all the blood along my
    veins,
And as with foul and poisonous vapor
    stains
The glad day's beauty, — though with
    anguish fraught
Our parting, I would fain be near, that
    nought
Might miss me of the swift and torturing
    pains
Such loss would nourish, — for my soul
    disdains
A peace of ignorance or oblivion bought.
And, Love! I would not be the first
    to go,
Lest thy dear eyes might drop a single
    tear,

Remembering one who worshipped them
    so well;
Or lest some sudden pang thy breast
    might know,
When, half forgetting, thou shouldst
    chance to hear
Some careless voice my name and story
    tell.

THINE EYES.

In other days, Belovèd, when the world
Has stepped between us, and thou
  seem'st to be
Far off, — when half effaced my memory
By mists of sweeter incense round thee
  curled
Than I can offer, — when, like dead
  leaves whirled
Before a storm, my glad dreams break
  and flee
Before relentless fate's reality —
When youth and joy their golden wings
  have furled —
Even then, O Love! I shall not quite
  despair;
Even then, upon my weary heart and
  sore
A gentle after-sunset glow will rise
And comfort me; some moments will be
  fair.

And looking back, I still shall smile once
    more,
Remembering the old kindness of thine
    eyes.

DEPENDENCE.

WHAT would life keep for me if thou
    shouldst go ?
Belovèd, give me answer : for my art
Is pledged unto thy service, and my
    heart
Apart from thee nor joy nor grace doth
    know.
No arid desert, no wide waste of snow,
Looks drearier to exiled ones who start
On their forced journey than, shouldst
    thou depart,
This fair green earth to my dead hope
    would show.
And like a drowning man who struggling
    clings
With stiffened fingers to the rope that
    saves,
Thrown out to meet his deep need from
    the land,
So to thy thought I hold when sorrow's
    wings

Darken the sky, and 'mid the bitterest
  waves
Of fate am succored by thy friendly
  hand.

SUBMISSION.

GOD forbid, dearest, that I should com-
    plain
However hard and heavy be the cross
Thou bidst me carry; since to me all
    loss
Incurred for thee turns straightway into
    gain,
And by the side of thine inflicted pain
All pleasure won from others is as dross
Beside pure gold. Like summer winds
    that toss
The branches of the trees whose trunks
    remain
Unmoved, so sweep the floods of cir-
    cumstance,
Ruffling alone the current of my mood,
While my soul's deep repose they can-
    not shake.
But at a word of thine, before thy glance,
My spirit bows, knowing thy will is good,
Eager to do or suffer for thy sake.

LOVE'S CALENDAR.

I TAKE no heed of month, or week, or
    day,
Or of the times and seasons of the year.
Springtime it is with me when she is
    near,
And winter when the clouds of absence
    stray
Across my heaven, holding its sun at
    bay.
The morning dawns when her dear eyes
    appear,
And night shuts down upon me, blank
    and drear,
When those consoling orbs are taken
    away.
As earth is gladdened when the snows
    depart,
When woods and meadows are no longer
    bare,
But tender blossoms nestle in the grass,

So, when my Love approaches, to my
    heart
Her balmy breath brings floods of sum-
    mer air,
And fresh flowers spring where'er her
    footsteps pass.

ISLANDS.

" Some unsuspected isle in far-off seas." — BROWNING.

BEYOND the sea-coast, where the level
    sea
Stretches its shining length, some isle
    must rest,
Cradled upon the ocean's bounteous
    breast,
Where men might live untrammelled,
    glad, and free.
Out of life's babbling current there must
    be
Some unsuspected isle, Love's dear be-
    quest
To those who follow him, where, safe
    and blest,
Oh ! my belovèd, I might dwell with
    thee.
But ships are not found strong enough
    to bear

Adventurers over every ocean's foam ;
Not all my thought, not all my love and
    care,
Can build the bark in which we two
    might roam ;
So still my voice assails the unheeding
    air
With vain lamentings for that island
    home.

SNOW-DROPS.

ALREADY once I 've brought you snow-
    drops, dear,
From an old garden whose forgotten
    grace
Seemed to revive again a little space
To do you honor. Though March winds
    blow drear
And chill, yet, with sweet sense that
    spring is near,
These brave and hardy buds the snow
    displace ;
Showing, each one, a white and shining
    face, —
The earliest flowers of the awakening
    year.
So, like the snow-drops, once for me
    there grew,
Amid the snows of life, pure blossoms,
    when

Your smile first rested on me, and I
    knew
My springtime was at hand. To-day,
    again,
The flowers of spring and love I bring
    to you,
With heart unchanged and faithful now
    as then.

LOVE'S ABODE.

Up the white steps that lead to Love's
    abode
I hastened, tarrying by the golden gate.
" Ruler of gods and men," I cried, " I
    wait
To pay my homage here where most 't is
    owed ! "
Then the bright gate swung open, and
    bestowed
An entrance, and Love's servants in
    sweet state
Came out to meet and welcome me.
    Elate
And proud, I followed where the way
    they showed :
They led me to the temple door, whence
    gleam
Soft lights, whence sweet scents float
    upon the air.

"Here wait our master's voice," they
    said, and then —
They left me.   When shall I be called,
    oh when,
Into the inner sanctuary, where,
Amid his chosen ones, Love reigns
    supreme ?

STORM AND CALM.

WHILE LISTENING TO A ST. SAËNS CON-
CERTO.

THE waves of love will dash me on a
shore
Trackless and waste, whence there is no
return.
My mast is split, my rudder gone ;
they burn
Like glowing coals, — these icy waves
that pour
Across my shattered deck ; the mad
winds tore
Long since my sails in shreds. The
black heavens yearn
To clasp the deep; no star can I dis-
cern
That might direct me till the storm were
o'er.
So rose the cry of one in agony,

Tossed on wide floods of passion, doubt,
    and dread.
Then, as a clear morn smiles upon the
    sea,
When a wild night has spread its wings
    and fled,
So thy sweet eyes arose and shone on
    me,
And peace and calm upon my soul were
    shed.

SERVING.

THAT thou 'rt not yet all mine why
    should I care ?
Why grieve because the draught is scant
    and thin
Which thy love offers for my tasting in
Its fragile cup, at moments short and
    rare ?
Fool should I be thus early to despair !
The labors of my love but now begin.
Twice seven long years did Jacob serve
    to win
Rachel, and dwelt with her long days
    and fair ;
So I will serve for thee ; from land to
    land
Gleaning and gathering, until twice seven
    years,
And more, if need be, on their path shall
    roll ;

With fond assurance that we two shall
    stand
At last, together, 'mid the blessèd
    spheres
Of love's domain, united soul to soul.

THE BURDEN OF LOVE.

I BEAR an unseen burden constantly ;
Waking or sleeping I can never thrust
The load aside ; through summer's heat
    and dust
And winter's snows it still abides with
    me.
I cannot let it fall though I should be
Never so weary ; carry it I must.
Nor can the bands that bind it on me
    rust
Or break, nor ever shall I be set free.
Sometimes 't is heavy as the weight that
    bore
Atlas on giant shoulders ; sometimes
    light
As the frail message of the carrier dove ;
But, light or heavy, shifting never more.
What is it thus oppressing, day and
    night ?
The burden, dearest, of a mighty love.

A SIMILE.

At sea, far parted from the happy shore,
The solitary rock lies all unmoved
By the caressing waves, though unre-
  proved
Their constant kisses on its breast they
  pour.
So it stands witnessed by all human
  lore,
Where'er the wanton god of love has
  roved,
His shafts fell never equal; one be-
  loved,
One lover, there must be for evermore.
Dear, if thou wilt, be thou that rock at
  sea,
But let me be the waves that never leave
Their yearning towards it through the
  ocean space;
And be thou the belovèd, but let me
Be the fond lover destined to receive
And hold thee in love's infinite embrace.

BLOSSOMS OF LOVE.

Suggested by Dante Rossetti's Sonnet, "Passion and Worship."

THE blossoms of my love are many-hued
And manifold : some glow like tongues
    of fire
With the hot dyes of passionate desire ;
And some are white as snow, and heavy-
    dewed
With fallen tears ; with modesty im-
    bued,
Some bow their heads ; some, purple-
    robed, aspire
To flaunt before the world their proud
    attire ;
Some, soberer tinted, blush in solitude.
And all these varied blooms I watch and
    tend
And guard with constant care, untir-
    ingly,
That they new grace and beauty may
    possess ;

And many a busy day and night I spend
In weaving of their wealth a crown for
    thee.
Belovèd, wilt thou wear it?   Answer
    yes.

DEPRECATION.

ESTRELLA TO ALFONSO.

A PALLID nun behind the iron bars
Of fate, I sit and watch the roses blow
That are for others with wan smiles ;
    and so
I hear thy song sweep past me to the
    stars.
Like haughty conquerors in triumphal
    cars,
Thy mad hopes ride within thy breast,
    and go
Dauntlessly into realms I do not know,
And my pale peace thy passion breaks
    and mars.
O friend ! cease, therefore, thy wild min-
    strelsy;
No chord responsive vibrates in my
    breast,

And its dead ashes stir not at thy call.
Then, for thy love's sake, since thou
      lovest me,
Silence the voice I may not answer, lest,
Striving to flee from it, I faint and fall.

NEPENTHE.

UNTO Telemachus, who, journeying,
 sought
At Menelaus' court tidings to hear
Of great Odysseus, tarrying year on
 year,
The fair-armed Helen sweet refreshment
 brought, —
Nepenthe, Eastern juice. Such charm
 it wrought
That whoso tasted it could shed no tear
A whole day long : though all he held
 most dear
Were struck with death, he knew and
 suffered naught.
So thou, a later Helen, bringest me
A draught wherein oblivion and repose
In cunning portions are together blent.
I drink : my tears are dry, my soul can
 see
No ill, and even sorrow's memory grows
Forgotten in a nameless, deep content.

ΣΥ ΣΩΤΗΡ.

A WISE and famous nation held belief,
Whoever in prosperity o'ergrew
The bounds of temperate good, him
    would pursue
The ever-jealous gods with loss and
    grief.
Sometimes so golden is my harvest's
    sheaf,
My way so flowery and my heaven so
    blue,
I tremble lest, perchance, the immortals
    brew
A storm to prove my fortune's sudden
    thief.
But thou art my preserver even here,
And earn'st me mercy from the envious
    skies ;
Since, lacking thee, I lack the one thing
    dear,

Which only were life's first and fairest
    prize ;
For other joys are barren all and drear,
Beside that one which a stern fate de-
    nies.

IN A LETTER.

THERE came a breath out of a distant
    time,
An odor from neglected gardens where
Unnumbered roses once perfumed the
    air
Through summer days, in childhood's
    happy clime.
There came the salt scent of the sea, the
    chime
Of waves against the beaches or the
    bare,
Gaunt rocks; as to the mind, half una-
    ware,
Recur the words of some familiar rhyme.
And as above the gardens and the sea
The moon arises, and her silver light
Touches the landscape with a deeper
    grace,

So o'er the misty wraiths of memory,
Turning them into pictures clear and
    bright,
Rose in a halo the belovèd face.

TITLES.

BORN sovereigns have no names but
those bestowed
In baptism; Constance, Philip, — so each
age
Knows them, and deals of praise or
blame their wage,
As harvests of good fame or ill they
sowed.
So with the mighty, o'er whose cradle
glowed
The star of genius; with that heritage
Dante and Raphael shine on history's
page
Simple as when they walked our common road.
Like thy great namesake, in whose cause
the plain
Of Troy was strewn with corpses, while
above

Olympus heard the wrathful gods con-
    tend,
So, 'mid the homage of respect and love
Laid at thy feet by lover and by friend,
Helen thou art, and Helen must remain.

AFTER ABSENCE.

AFTER long years of absence had gone
    by,
He stood again upon the parent shore
Of stern New England; but his heart
    was sore,
And his dulled bosom rent with many a
    sigh.
He mourned the vanished gods, the ra-
    diant sky
Of the dear land of love and song and
    lore ;
He mourned the sweet companionships
    of yore,
That on his path like scattered pearls
    did lie.
But when she passed, as in the former
    days,
With the old halo on her golden hair,
With the old kindness and enchanting
    ways,

'T was as if some swift wind had cleared
  the air;
Before her smile he stood transfixèd
  there;
He had forgotten that she was so fair.

BONDAGE.

"AND this is freedom!" cried the serf;
    "At last
I tread free soil, the free air blows on
    me;"
And, wild to learn the sweets of liberty,
With eager hope his bosom bounded
    fast.
But not for naught had the long years
    amassed
Habit of slavery; among the free
He still was servile, and, disheartened,
    he
Crept back to the old bondage of the
    past.
Long did I bear a hard and heavy chain
Wreathèd with amaranth and asphodel,
But through the flower-breaths stole the
    weary pain.
I cast it off and fled, but 't was in vain;
For when once more I passed by where
    it fell,
I took it up and bound it on again.

WITCH-HAZEL.

'T IS said that 'mid the sylvan shrubs
    that grow
One has a wizard power above the rest;
Held o'er the soil it points its leafy
    crest
To where the hidden sources sleep be-
    low.
How must the gentle earth rejoice when
    flow
The pent-up streams and ease the aching
    breast,
Grown sore with guarding them! And
    ah, how blest
Those springs to men who need of water
    know!
Belovèd, at thy touch the entire bliss
Of being floods me; in my heart straight-
    way
Songs rise and gush and murmur with-
    out end.

And, dear, who knows but that, per-
    chance, some day,
Some one may be a little glad for this
That thou hast wrought, and bless thee
    through thy friend ?

CALM.

See H. H.'s Sonnet, " The Zone of Calms."

HERE let us rest within "the zone of
    calms,"
Found now at last, whose delicate mys-
    teries
Escaped us on the old tempestuous
    seas,
Though *their* best gifts this charmèd
    space embalms.
Here are soft shadows as of darkling
    palms,
Whose branches faintly rustle in the
    breeze
Of summer morns, and gentle melodies
As of hushed voices chanting low sweet
    psalms.
The tyrant Time, plying his ceaseless
    oar,
Will bear us farther all too soon, we
    know, —
Eastward and westward, parted as be-
    fore.

But while we linger yet, each opposite
 shore
Still indistinct, take speech, O Love,
 once more,
And bless the rapturous stillness ere we
 go !

SYMPHONIE FANTASTIQUE.

WE heard the symphony wherein the
    brain
Of the mad poet fancies his love to be
A sweet, ever-recurring melody,
Piquing to pleasure, ministering to pain.
Now ball-rooms echo it, now wood and
    plain
Take up the burden ; joyous now and
    free
It sounds, now sad and fraught with
    mystery :
All life is interwoven with that strain.
Thou art the melody of all my days,
I but an accidental note in thine,
Its value unobserved by alien ears.
Remove it, still thy music is as fine ;
But take thee from me, and the void dis-
    plays
Discord and inharmonious fall of tears.

IDEM NON ALITER.

SAY not the charm is broken ; that the old
Rapture has faded to a cool content ;
That flowers so sweet at morn *must* lose
    their scent,
When toward life's noon experience shall
    have rolled.
Nor whisper that the tale so often told
Fails in some measure of its blandish-
    ment ;
Nor that the chord jangles wherein were
    blent
All harmonies that music's voices hold.
Ah, dear, a shining isle forever lies
Beyond the track of ships, in the still sea,
Where chains are hid in wooing, soft
    disguise.
More blest than freedom seems captiv-
    ity ;
For the old Circe looks from out thine
    eyes,
And thy Odysseus does not wish to flee.

THE SLEEPING BEAUTY.

I.

GUARDED by walls of roses set with
    thorns,
Within her palace-room the princess
    slept,
Nor heard how through the wood the
    loud chase swept,
With bay of hounds and note of hunt-
    ing-horns.
Into some dream of summer eves and
    morns
Perchance a sudden thrill prophetic
    crept,
As to her side one eager hunter leapt,
Made strong by love that bans and bar-
    riers scorns.
Before his tread, — as at some sharp
    blade's stroke
A flower might fall, — the deep enchant-
    ment broke.

He pressed his lips to hers in love's long
    kiss;
And as her name in rapturous tone he
    spoke,
With happy, smiling eyes the princess
    woke
To meet the new and unsuspected bliss.

II.

Once more in slumbering state a princess
    lay,
While in the shadow of her palace-walls
Unheeded died the glad and pleading
    calls
Of love and joy the outer world that
    sway.
But when towards evening sped her
    peaceful day.
Despite a charm that soul and sense en-
    thralls,
Into the stillness of her perfumed halls,
On fire with love, I made my venturous
    way.
Lo! I have waked her with my ardent
    lips;

Have seen the warm blood mantle in her
    cheek
That surged impetuous round my own
    heart's core.
Yet once again she sank in sleep's
    eclipse.
Oh, be more powerful now the word I
    speak,
The touch I give! Sweet princess, sleep
    no more!

FRIENDSHIP AND LOVE.

FRIENDSHIP sat smiling on a flowery
    height,
Watching the blooming groves, the
    meadows green,
The peaceful stream that flowed the
    fields between.
"How rich my realm," she breathed,
    "how glad, how bright!"
But on a sudden fell a purple-light,
Deepening the tranquil beauty of the
    scene,
Tingeing with amethyst hue the river's
    sheen,
As Love drew near in majesty and
    might.
"This is my kingdom, sister!" quick
    he cried.
"My paths are not all stormy; there
    is calm

Upon my mountains, and clear skies
    above.
This radiant land thou viewest bears *my*
    balm,
Profounder far than thine." Then
    Friendship sighed,
But rose, and yielded up her seat to
    Love.

THE TROUBADOUR.

Thou Troubadour, roaming from land
    to land,
Singing, indeed, we grant, one endless
    theme, —
Thy lady's praise, — and striving to re-
    deem
The pledges laid on thee by Love's com-
    mand,
We are the truer lovers, we who stand
Beside our mistress, though no silver
    stream
Of song escape our lips. Thou art the
    dream,
We the realities her eyes have scanned.
" Know ye," he answered, " how those
    lilies grow
That on the lake's breast seem to float
    apart
And free, though fastened firm their
    roots below ?

Thus do I seem before the wind and
    tide
Of chance and change to sway from
    side to side ;
But still my heart is anchored to her
    heart."

"THE GREEK YOUTH."

"HE goes," she said: "there, at the
    opening door,
I see a shimmer as of snowy wings;
'T is his white robe that as he passes
    flings
Its shining undulation o'er the floor." *
But while she spoke, his fond arms as
    before
Held her, his kiss burned on her lips;
    as sings
Some woodland bird, his voice's mur-
    murings
Thrilled with the joyous weight of love
    he bore.
'T was but the moonlight of thine own
    sad eyes
That cast my shadow; in thy silver
    sphere,
Half dusk, half light, ghosts start at any
    breath.

I bring the sunshine ; in it no surprise
Can come, no shade can walk.   Lo! I
    am here,
Belovèd, and shall be here unto death.

WANDERLEBEN.

HE has no home, he owns no father-
    land;
His country is the hospitable earth.
He shapes his course where, past the
    fields of dearth,
The planet's greenest groves of plenty
    stand;
But howsoever golden be the strand
He treadeth, clearer than the sound of
    mirth
And laughter steals the voice that still
    gives birth
To his best joy, more potent than com-
    mand.
Again and once again his ship he steers
Into one harbor, hastening to the saint
Before whose shrine his constant offer-
    ing glows.
He heaps his treasure, won with blood
    and tears,

There at her feet ; praying, without com-
plaint,
Leave but to worship as he comes and
goes.

HER ROSES.

AGAINST her mouth she pressed the
    rose, and there,
'Neath the caress of lips as soft and red
As its own petals, quick the bright bud
    spread
And oped, and flung its fragrance on the
    air.
It ne'er again a bud's young grace can
    wear?
O love, regret it not! It gladly shed
Its soul for thee, and though thou kiss
    it dead
It does not murmur at a fate so fair.
Thus, once, thou breath'dst on me, till
    every germ
Of love and song broke into rapturous
    flower,
And sent a challenge upwards to the
    sky.

What if too swift fruition set a term
Too brief to all things? I have lived
    my hour,
And die contented, since for thee I die.

AT THE CONVENT.

I CANNOT pass beyond the jealous gate
And the high walls that, rising stern and
    grim,
Shut you, like sullen guards, within the
    dim
Mysterious space no man may penetrate.
But I can guess how the gray nuns
    chide : " Late
Thou comest, sister ; still thy lamp 's to
    trim.
Thy clear voice failed us in the evening
    hymn
Wherewith the grace of Heaven we sup-
    plicate."
Dear, as some paltry coin a lady might
Fling to appease a beggar, ere you go
Into your quiet cell and all is night,
Tarry a moment at the casement ; throw
The guerdon of your smile, his way to
    light,
On your poor errant minstrel down be-
    low.

FAUST AND HELENA.

I.

WHEN all that life contains of rich and
    good,
Being his own, had failed to bring con-
    tent
To Faust, there rose the form wherein
    were blent
All graces of all beauty's sisterhood :
Victorious Helen, young as when first
    wooed
By Theseus : lovely as when heroes bent
Their steps to death, and seas of blood
    were spent,
To win her, fairest of the heavenly
    brood.
But from his longing arms, that thus at
    last
Embraced the shade of beauty and were
    blest,

She fled to pale Persephone's domain.
Oh, risen again, sweet spirit! let the past
Yield to the present; here upon my breast
Forget the courts that wait for thee in vain.

II.

As unto Faust, when all life holds had failed
To bring content, the Beauteous One returned,
Summoned from Hades, at whose sight gods burned,
And goddesses with sudden envy paled,
So, when the banquet of this world regaled
My spirit poorly, all for which it yearned
Rose in thy presence, and my eyes discerned
In thine the whole of loveliness unveiled.
But from his clasping arms the vision fled
Back to the silent realms, and once more left

Him lone, unsatisfied, and desolate.
Sweet, vanish never, lest my heart,
    bereft,
Consume itself with longing for its dead
Delight, and to despair be consecrate.

TWO FIGURES.

One, like a creature born of brighter
    spheres
Than these we know, a child of joy and
    light,
Brought gladness, beauty, and love's
    blessèd might,
Worship and praise and reverence shorn
    of fears.
And one, receiving all that most endears
Soul unto soul, and maketh sweet the
    sight
Of him that gives, the offering to re-
    quite,
Placed in the other's hand an urn of
    tears.
Love veiled his brows, and would have
    fled; but lo !
There came a whisper from the giver's
    breast

That stayed his fluttering wings and held
    him back :
" Upon my head these gathered tears
    bestow
A great and softening grace it else would
    lack, —
The crown of sorrow.   Dear, thy gift is
    best."

SERVICE.

Show me some way in which my soul
    may serve
Thy soul, its nourisher; teach me to
    say
Some word to ease thy heart with, or to
    lay
Soothing upon a sore and startled nerve;
Let me aspire to lend some gracious
    curve
To the straight lines dividing day from
    day;
Help me to hold the errant feet that
    stray
In paths of constancy that never swerve.
Sometimes I fail to reach thee, the
    ascent
Being so steep to where thou dwell'st;
    in vain
My hands are rich with gifts thou canst
    not take.

But could I see my life blood, for thy
      . sake,
To profit thee, flow in a crimson stain,
Dear, I believe that I could die content.

COMMUNION.

ONE cannot draw the bars against the
    friends
And guests that crowd for entrance at
    his gate;
He opes, inviting, nor the simple state
Of his abode against their train defends.
But there are chambers where the lover
    tends
His sacred fires; where no feet pene-.
    trate,
Save of immortals; where, early and
    late,
The breath of prayer and sacrifice as-
    cends.
In such a spot as this, as in the shrine
Of some white temple, in a dusk made
    sweet
With incense, far from outer noise and
    heat,

And hollow haste of them that part and
    meet,
Surrounded by dim presences divine,
My soul communes eternally with thine.

MISCELLANEOUS.

IMPATIENCE.

I SEE the ships go sailing, sailing ;
  My feet are fettered to the shore.
  Their prows with many a voyage are
      hoar.
See ! on the far horizon paling,
  They sink and are no more.

I see the birds go flying, flying ;
  In swaying line and whirling ring,
  'Twixt blue and blue, their way they
      wing ;
But the swift flocks, through ether ply-
      ing,
  To me no message bring.

I see the moon go riding, riding,
  Through heavenly paths, on golden
      wheels ;
  Her passing kiss the ocean feels,
But, in his bosom swiftly hiding
  His joy, no word reveals.

O golden moon, and snowy pinions
 Of birds that fly and ships that mate
 Their speed with birds, in royal state
Sweep proudly through your wide do-
  minions !
 And I, — I only wait.

IM FREIEN.

Ich gehe immer und schweige:
　Dort oben ein Vöglein singt;
Und durch die Fichtenzweige
　Die freundliche Sonne dringt.

Die Blumen blühn auf den Wiesen,
　Die Lüfte wandelnd gehn;
Weit in der Ferne, wie Riesen,
　Die hohen Gebirge stehn.

Die lieblichen Schatten liegen
　Auf der Erde kühler Brust;
Die weissen Wolken fliegen
　Im Himmel und tanzen vor Lust.

Oh! schöne, theure Erde,
　Du ziehst mich an dein Herz
Mit lockender Geberde;
　Verschwunden ist jeder Schmerz.

Verschwunden sind Wehen und Leiden,
  Vergessen Eile und Hast;
Es wecken nur Wonne und Freuden;
  Es bleiben nur Ruhe und Rast.

PROPITIATION.

A FRESH wind blows against the land :
    The crested waves toss to and fro ;
The swelling waves and shining sand
    Glitter like rifts of frozen snow.

The breath of morn lies soft and dim
    Upon the sea ; the tender trace
Of pink along the horizon's rim
    Her lips left in the azure space.

So on the threshold of the morn,
    Before the unclosing door I wait ;
Will hope expire ?   Will joy be born ?
    How stands it in the book of fate ?

O august sisters, sisters three,
    Who hold the distaff, spin the thread,
And weave all human destiny
    Into a pattern bright or dread,

9

I ask no boon of you ; desire
 And fear ye know ; I only bring
In words that morning hours inspire
 Propitiatory offering.

And though no altars rise apart
 Where men your awful praise re-
  hearse,
I build an altar in my heart,
 And on it lay my pleading verse.

MUSA LOQUITUR.

CHILD ! thine aspiring sense divines,
  Doubtless, the voice that speaks to
    thee.
  Arise ! across yon tossing sea
A path of light and glory shines.

It leads unto the fields of art,
  Whose golden harvests thou may'st
    reap,
  And 'mid thy garnered treasures keep,
If humble and devout of heart.

Go, dwell with gods and heroes ; learn
  The lessons mighty marbles teach,
  And of the laurel-crowned their
    speech
That through the centuries doth burn.

Then lowly kneel at Nature's feet,
  And from her beating bosom draw
  Wisdom, without whose perfect law
The best of art were incomplete.

Listen, in climes of warmth and light,
　To the sweet-throated nightingales.
　Watch, till the morn's embrace pre-
　　vails,
The starry splendors of the night.

On shores where placid waters roll,
　Invite the breezes of the South,
　Till their fleet kisses pass thy mouth
And penetrate thine inmost soul.

Then, when thy voice grows full and
　　strong,
　When all within, without, is fair,
　Pierce with thy call the expectant air,
And wake thy lyre to Lesbian song.

WAKING.

I WOKE once more.
 The spherèd ocean-spaces lay,
Empty and vast, behind, before,
 Where we must blindly trace our way
From unknown shore to unknown shore.

The moon's cold gleam
 Was faint with morn ; the stars had
   paled ;
But chanting one incessant theme
 Of loss and sorrow, they bewailed
The fading of my happy dream.

O bitter sea,
 They cried, whereon he floats alone
And joyless, now his dream and he
 Have parted, whose divine light shone
Cresting the waves of memory !

O envious fate,
 Whose ruthless hand the vision tore,
And robbed his bosom of the freight
 So dear, so matchless, that it bore,
And left it bare and desolate !

So swelled the song
 From star to star ; and like a stain
Upon the morning, rolled along
 The sea the echo of the strain,
Ceaseless regret for grief and wrong.

But then my heart
 That strove for courage, and would
  hide,
If that might be, in smiles its smart,
 With words half true, half false, re-
  plied :
Of man's great load each lifts his part.

And why despair ?
 Surely these morning clouds shall
  change
To evening clouds, and they will bear
 Fresh dreams along their fleecy range, .
And with new landscapes paint the air,

Until the last
  Deep sleep, when over all the woes
Of love and life the earth is cast,
  And, stilled in absolute repose,
Dreaming and waking both are past.

THE ROSE AND THE STATUE.

THE Rose said to the Statue : Thou art
  cold
  And passionless, though beautiful
    and grand.
  I all my life exhale, while thou dost
    stand
Unmoved, unmindful of the sweets I
  hold.

The Statue answered to the Rose : Thou
  poor,
  Frail creature, toy and wanton of a
    day,
  I scarce can stoop to note thy swift
    decay ;
Lo ! thou art fading *now*, but *I* endure.

Thus each reproached the other : neither
  thought
  What various means lead to an end
    the same ;

How manifold is beauty, and what
claim
To the world's gratitude the other
brought.

O Statue ! shine in majesty, replete
With high suggestions of eternal
things.
O Rose! yield up thy breath and die ;
the wings
Of love receive it, for thy breath is
sweet.

One must be cold and suffer, — 't is
earth's blight ;
One must be warm and suffer. Thus
the poles
Touch in a law unchanging ; but the
souls
Of Statue and of Rose can ne'er unite.

WONDERS.

TO E. B.

It is a wonder when the day
   Breaks from the portals of the night,
   And with her joyous smile and bright,
Crowns the high hills where darkness
      lay,
   And floods the outstretching plains
      with light.

A wonder when the bud perceives
   How tight its petals press, and grows
   Impatient of control, and throws,
Nourished by dews of morns and eves,
   Wide in the air the perfect rose.

Or when the gilded butterfly
   Wakes from the sleep in which were
      furled
   The joyous wings about him curled ;

And breaks the shell, and, floating high,
   Goes on his glad way through the
     world.

But greater marvels even than these
   Are such as harbor in the soul,
   Like words within some fast-sealed
     scroll,
Concealing close what mysteries!
   Till strikes the hour, and they unroll;

When eyes once cold, that looked
     askance,
   Kindle at ours, and send a ray
   Of warmth and cheer along our way,
And with their deep and tender glance
   Herald the dawn of love's new day;

When lips we never thought to taste
   Thrill 'neath our own; when fond
     arms reach
   About us; when quick heart-beats
     teach
How burns the breast we hold em-
     braced, —
   Love's signs more eloquent than
     speech.

When these things are, should we not
    lift
    The heart to Heaven with thankful
        prayer
    That, working wonders everywhere,
It wrought for us this gracious gift,
    Than which no other is more fair?

Dear, while I whisper, bend thy cheek
    A little nearer; where my strong
    Deep praise and sweet new joy belong
Thou know'st; the sense of what I speak,
    The happy secret of my song.

IN MEMORIAM.

B. H. C.

AT SORRENTO.

I.

THE Summer strews with lavish hand
   Her gems upon this Southern shore ;
With gold and emeralds glows the land,
   And sapphires form the ocean's floor.

The sun a glittering ruby gleams ;
   Each star a topaz ; while the mist
That o'er the mountain summits streams
   Is set with many an amethyst.

Unto the evening's gates of pearl
   There leads an opal-pavèd way,
And pearly are the clouds that curl
   About the bosom of the day.

But oft upon the radiant scene
   Thy image, O my friend, appears,
And all the jewels that have been
   Are changed to diamonds in my tears.

II.

With   flowers   and   lights   the   altars
   blazed ;
The   white-robed   priests,   with   crosses
   raised
And banners fluttering, onward came
'Mid many a candle's flickering flame.
The gentle dusk its mantle wrapped
About the landscape ; quiet lapped
The land, until the pious throng
Uplifted a thanksgiving song.

Then, held on high, that over all
With equal light its rays might fall,
And equal grace to all afford,
Was borne the Body of the Lord.
And, at its sight, upon their knees
The people fell as when a breeze
Sweeps o'er the summer earth at morn,
Bowing a field of uncut corn.

Why should thy spirit seem to shine
Here, where a creed so unlike thine
Lavished the treasures of its art,
And through the senses touched the
    heart ?
I know not ; but as with the rest
I knelt, thy memory dear and blest,
A living presence seemed to be,
And sacred grew the hour to me.

FROM NAPLES TO ROME.

THE sun set ; the wide Campagna
   Stretched about us like a sea,
Miles on miles of billowy distance ;
   Scarce a limit seemed to be
   To the great immensity,

Till upon the far horizon,
   Through the mist the hills rose
      higher,
And upon three tallest summits,
   Shooting, like a golden spire,
   Heavenwards, blazed a beacon fire.

And we knew that in the evening
   Stillness, where the eternal dome
Rises over tower and palace,
   Lay our long-desired home, —
   Lay the great enchantress, Rome.

Watch-fires kindled by the ages,
  Where the passing moments pour
All the present's shifting fuel
  On the accumulated store
  Till the pile glows more and more,

To the grand and wondrous precincts
  Of her hoary walls invite.
And, with longing for the morning
  To reveal them to our sight,
  Grateful hearts thanked God that
    night.

GIARDINO GIUSTI.

CLAD in a garb of centuries,
  Like solemn warders of the past,
  Above its secret hoards amassed,
Stand the funereal cypress-trees.

And each to each they nod and wave,
  And whisper how the king of kings
  Is death, and how all human things
Bloom but to wither in the grave.

But, down below, the city lies,
  Near where the shining river runs
  Within whose breast a thousand suns
Are mirrored from the cloudless skies.

And crowded market-place and square
  And street with fluttering flags are
    gay,
  And all the glad life of to-day
Pulses and surges everywhere.

For 'neath the Past's almighty shade
  The careless Present keeps its cheer;
  And though the end is sure and near,
Yet we press onward undismayed.

VERONA, *December*, 1878.

FOUNTAINS IN ROME.

Before St. Peter's, like the wreaths
  Of spotless snow that o'er the bare
Sad earth the pitying winter breathes,
  The proud jets flash into the air.
But where the water breaks and falls
  And meets the sun, with every gem
It glows wherewith shall deck her walls
  One day the new Jerusalem.

While here, beside a mighty pile
  Where spoils of splendid ages gleam,
The Triton, with an endless smile,
  Uplifts to heaven his slender stream.
And there Bernini's grotesque taste
  With nymphs and gods the square
    adorns ;
And giant groups in circle placed
  Fill the wide basins from their horns.

Here Trevi, whose enchanted pool,
  When hearts with parting anguish
    burn,

Will yield in draughts divinely cool
  Consoling promise of return ;
Where come the doves to bathe and
    drink,
  And seek for shade amid the glare
Of noon, beneath the fountain's brink,
  Or 'mid the mermen's clustering hair.

But these, the body's thirst that slake,
  That pour in many a loved retreat
Their fresh and limpid floods, and make
  The beauty of the Roman street,
Seem but the images of those
  Deep sources 'mid the city's span
That in their hoary breasts enclose
  The wondrous history of man.

Rome ! of these fountains of thy lore
  Let my soul drink.   Not all in vain
Be oped for me thy matchless store,
  Nor closed without return again.
Let some sweet stream of tuneful praise
  Towards thy clear heaven its voice
    uplift,
Along whose flow shall shine and blaze
  The gracious rainbow of thy gift.

A ROMA.

Città delle città!
Nel tuo cielo chiaro, ridente,
Splende il sole col più bel folgor;
Sul tuo suolo dove la storia
Spande la piena del suo tesor,
Brillan uniti l'antica gloria
E del presente
Tutti i fior.

Città delle città!
Mentre il fiume corre in fretta,
Che della vita si suol chiamar,
Pallide ombre fra il tuo bello
Spazio tornan a dimorar,
E del tranquillo e calmo avello
Che ci aspetta
A favellar.

Città delle città!
La tua fronte porta la soma

D'ogni delizia e d'ogni desir ;
Nel tuo seno contempliamo
Giunti il riso e il sospir ;
Sul tuo cuore impariamo
  A viver, oh ! Roma,
  E a morir.

ON THE PINCIAN.

THEIR dusky boughs the pine-trees lift
   Against the heaven's transcendent
      hue;
Nor does the faintest cloudlet drift
   One film across the perfect blue.
The world lies bathed in sunshine; hill
   And hollow, fountain, circling stream,
Sparkle with light, and hushed and still
   The city, like a dream.

So smiles the Present, while the Past,
   Mysterious, dim, about it lies,
Guarding the kingdoms wide and vast,
   Invisible to human eyes;
But whispering to human ears,
   With speech more potent than our
      own,
The story of the by-gone years,
   In low, perpetual tone.

It tells how soon the race was o'er
   For others ; how we soon shall be,
With kings and emperors gone before,
   But shadows of reality ;
And how we pass that they may come
   Whom Time's swift courses bear
      along;
How other lips, when ours are dumb,
   Shall blossom into song :

As now we sing beside their graves
   Whose rhythmic laughter once made
      glad
The earth, whose gentle memory craves
   From us more tender words than sad ;
And as to-day o'er quick and dead
   Extends the sky's unsullied space,
So ever o'er us all shall spread
   The infinite embrace ;

That change is not ; that destiny
   Rules with a calm, impartial sway ;
That to all eyes is given to see
   The generous beauty of the day.
And, last sweet comfort unto men, —
   The thought an armor 'gainst de-
      spair, —

Since this world is so blest, shall, then,
  A future be less fair?

With thoughts like these of peace and
      rest,
  Amid the noon's effulgent light,
Is soothed, not terrified, the breast,
  With shadows of the coming night;
And here within the soul's true home,
  Beneath thy calm and tranquil sky,
While making life all joy, O Rome,
  Thou teachest how to die.

AFTERMATH.

J. W., DIED MARCH, 1879.

BRAVE Heart, grown cold, didst thou
    not know
  Full recognition when the field
  Was green in June, and glad to yield
Its wealth to them who come to mow?

And were there some who doubted,
    some,
  Unwitting that perchance thy peer
  Moved not in distant ranks or near,
Upon whose lips thy praise grew dumb?

Such is the meed of genius, such
  Experience proves the frequent fate
  That 'mid the small attends the great;
They, bringing little, sneer at much.

But the late summer cometh, when
   Once more his scythe the reaper sets,
   And for the season's store-house gets
A new sweet crop to profit men.

So they as yet unborn shall reap
   The harvests of thy steadfastness
   And thy soul's noble law, and bless
The mighty " fruits of them that sleep."

A PRAYER.

Not through my merits but your grace,
  Immortal powers that set me free,
I stand before you face to face,
  And share in your eternity.

I know beyond this path so fair
  And joyous opes the dark abyss ;
I know that wreck and ruin there
  May be the end of too much bliss.

But spare me ! If my humble dread
  Appease the Fate yourselves obey,
Oh, on my bowed but crownèd head
  Let not your shafts descend to slay !

Your altars all I light with fires
  Where deepest awe and reverence
      meet ;
And garlanded with gained desires
  I cling, still suppliant, to your feet.

XAIPE!

HAIL and farewell! Thus in our brief
    career
  The greetings follow; for our paths
    unite
But to diverge, and those so near and
    dear
  To-day to-morrow vanish out of sight.

But, brave and patient heart, feel no
    dismay ;
  For though they pass as 't were be-
    hind a veil,
Thy dear ones are not lost, but all thy
    way
  Is gladdened with their voices crying
    Hail !

And when thou standest on the shadowy
    brink
  Of the profound Unknown, thy part-
    ing knell

Shall be their psalm of love, and thou
    shalt sink
  On sleep's soft breast, soothed by
    their fond farewell!

SCHUMANN'S SYMPHONY IN B FLAT MAJOR.

A TRUMPET-CALL the slumbering sense
  awakes,
And challenges to action and to fight.
But swift the plumèd line of battle
  breaks,
  And, breathing o'er the brows of love
   alight,
The rhythm, adrift with human joys and
  woes,
  Goes wandering with a question and a
   sigh
  Throughout all life's expectancy, to
   die
At last in notes of rapture, as it rose.
  The patriot Swiss, who clasped the
   hostile spears,
And through his bleeding breast carved
  freedom's way,

Had known his peer on many a glorious
    day,
  Had Schumann's muse been born of
    earlier years ;
For when such strains as these the
    heart do greet,
Great deeds seem easy, and to die were
    sweet.

JOACHIM.

Across the strings the sympathetic bow
Swept, held and guided by a master-
    hand.
Like the enchanted beauty long ago
Who slumbered, chained by magic bar
    and band,
Till on her lips the appointed prince did
    press
The liberating kiss and she awoke,
So, 'neath the bow's long-drawn desired
    caress,
Swift into full and perfect being broke,
Freed from the violin, the prisoned
    tones :
In myriad measure swelled the melody,
Bewailing now with sobs and broken
    moans
The bondage past, now joyous to be
    free :
And as the strain began to rise and roll,
The soul of music met the artist's soul.

RUBINSTEIN.

AMID expectant silence. grave and still,
He laid his hands upon the pallid keys.
Straightway the notes began to throb and
  thrill.
Mirrored in sound the mighty mysteries,
The fathomless of human life, its needs
And hopes. doubts, fears, fancies and
  questionings
Appeared, and last the tramp of funeral
  steeds,
And trappings of the grave.   On mighty
  wings
Uprose the stirring chords till the great
  dead
Heard where they wandered on the
  shadowy way.
Hushed for a moment was their solemn
  tread,

And athwart space a whisper seemed to
    stray, —
Hail! great interpreter of god-like men!
Beneath thy quickening touch we live
    again.

CHOPIN.

THE polonaise is danced; the waltz is
    done;
The guests are gone; but still the vague
    regret
That breathed through all things since
    the fête begun,
Waits, and unrest and longing linger
    yet.
Into the night! there lie repose and
    peace.
Hark! how the wandering voices meet
    and flow
In rhythm; hear now those calm accords
    and low,
Like dim forebodings of a swift release.
"Whom the gods love die young." So,
    Chopin, thou
Heard'st early, through the harmonies
    that stirred
Thy poet brain, the inevitable "Now!"

Mad'st answer, smiling, to the summon-
ing word,
And, sung to sleep on Music's tender
breast,
Sank'st gladly into an untroubled rest.

"MEIN TAG WAR HEITER, GLÜCKLICH MEINE NACHT."

FROM HEINE.

My day was joyous, happy was my night.
My people's plaudits rang whene'er the
    lyre
Of poesy I struck ; my song's sweet fire
Has kindled many a flame intense and
    bright.
My summer blossoms still, but piled
    and stored
Within my barns have I each golden ear
Of corn, and all that made the world so
    dear
Now must I leave — leave all I so
    adored.
The hand falls from the harp-strings ;
    shattered lie
The fragments of the glass with life re-
    plete,

That gayly on my haughty lips I pressed.
O God ! how hateful-bitter 't is to die !
O God ! how heavenly 't is to live, how
    sweet,
In this enchanting little earthly nest !

TO R. W. E.

As sweeps a wind at morning, cool and
    clear,
Against the wavering mists that break
    and flee,
Leaving the wide blue prairies of the sea
Outstretched in sunlit splendor far and
    near;
As, in the early breeze's fresh embrace,
The autumn flowers shake off their sleep
    and shine,
Gold, purple, 'mid a blaze of scarlet vine,
And all the fields are clothed with joy
    and grace, —
So, loftiest Teacher! sweep thy wingèd
    words
Against the mists and errors of our
    days.
So to thy voice respond a thousand
    chords
That slumbered, thrilling to perfected
    praise.

And 'neath the breath of thine inspiring
    mood,
The soul grows strong and life seems
    sweet and good.

CHAUCER.

A LIMPID source, a clear and bubbling
    spring,
Born in some wooded dell unknown of
    heat,
Above whose breast the leafy branches
    meet
And kiss, and earthward wavering shad-
    ows fling ;
Upon whose brink the perfumed flower-
    cups swing
'Neath the light tread of hurrying insect
    feet ;
Such, Chaucer, seems the sturdy note
    and sweet
In thine unfettered song reëchoing.
Hence they who sometimes weary of the
    play
Of fountains and the artificial jets
Which in gay parks and gardens dance
    and leap,

Turn back again into that forest-way
Where thy fresh stream the grass and
    mosses wets
That slumber on its margin cool and
    deep.

AT SEA.

WHAT lies beyond the far horizon's
    rim?
Ah! could our ship but reach and an-
    chor there,
What wondrous scenes, what visions
    bright and fair
Would meet the eyes that gazed across
    the brim!
But though we crowd the canvas on and
    trim
Our barque with skill, the proud waves
    seem to bear
No nearer to that goal, and everywhere
Stretches an endless circle wide and
    dim.
So do we dream, treading the narrow
    path
Of life, between the bounds of day and
    night,

To-morrow turns this page so often
  conned :
But when to-morrow cometh, lo ! it hath
The limits of to-day, and in its light
Still lies far off the unknown heaven be-
  yond.

II.

We sail the centre of a ceaseless round,
Forever circled by the horizon's rim ;
And fondly deem that from that far-off
  brim
Some sign will rise or some glad tidings
  sound.
But no word comes, nor aught to break
  the bound
Of sea and sky all day with distance
  dim,
And vanished quite when darkness, chill
  and grim,
About the deep her sable shroud has
  wound.
So on the seas of life and time we drift,
Within the circling limits of our fate,
Expectant ever of some solving breath.
But no sound comes, no pitying hand
  doth lift

The veil nor faith nor love can pene-
    trate,
And to our dusk succeeds the dark of
    death.

A VOYAGE.

" My soul is an enchanted boat." — SHELLEY.

LET us float on the downward-flowing
    stream,
Like to a happy lover with his bride.
My heart is still, my soul is satisfied,
Since thou art the companion of my
    dream.
Above our heads the golden planets
    gleam,
Fields strewn with flowers stretch by the
    river's side,
The rippling waves make music as we
    glide ;
Life, love and gladness is that music's
    theme.
Whence did we come into this magic
    boat ?
We know not, neither whither we are
    bound.

For fate is silent and its end unseen.
Let us float on — what should we do but
    float ?
Until we pass into some sea profound
Where all shall be as if it had not been.

12

KINGS.

"The real king that God makes is the man who melts all wills into his own."   CARLYLE.

I READ of kings and princes, how they
    sought
With flattering word and deed to hold
    the dower
Their sires bequeathed, and with new
    grants of power
The sufferance of the half-freed nations
    bought.
How vain and foolish is their race, I
    thought,
Who strut upon the stage their little
    hour,
Yet, like the meanest mortal, in the
    flower
Of pride and pomp, must perish and be
    naught.
Then fell the seër's words across my
    page:

The only king and sovereign by God's
      grace,
Is he who melts all wills into his own.
When this one comes to claim his heri-
      tage,
How we fall back to give the monarch
      place,
And bend the obedient knee before his
      throne !

WEAVING.

THE fair-armed Helen in her fragrant
    room
In Priam's palace, while the bloody
    fight
Raged in the plain below, beyond her
    sight,
Worked at a purple garment on the
    loom.
Into the web she wove pictures of gloom
And glory, deeds of prowess and of
    might,
Labors of Greeks and Trojans till black
    night
Enwrapt them and they came upon their
    doom.
Thus on the spreading loom of Time we
    weave
The garment of our life; the web we
    crowd
With shifting images by fate allowed

To fill from nothingness our short re-
    prieve ;
And haste the work although so loth to
    leave
What, being finished, serves us for a
    shroud.

A SHATTERED GLASS.

Among the curious trifles travellers
    show,
Are bits of flashing, rainbow-tinted
    glass,
Dropped by the hand of Time, that in
    the grass
Of seldom-trodden fields half-hidden
    glow.
What cups and bowls they fashioned
    who may know ?
But tales they tell to the new men that
    pass
Of old-time feasts and revels, and, alas !
Of pride and joy that perished long ago.
That was a beauteous vase from which
    we drank
Sunshine and smiles and love's sweet
    potion till
From hands too weak to bear its weight
    it sank,

And its frail rainbows shattered.   If you
    will,
Let us take up the fragments while we
    thank
A gracious Heaven that these are left
    us still.

SURPLUS.

With fullest sunshine that yon heaven
  reveals
Glittered the temple-walls of his abode;
And life on him those richest gifts be-
  stowed
Which else with niggard hand it most
  conceals.
The obstacles at which the faint soul
  feels
Its strength give way, were crushed,
  when not the goad
To new success, like pebbles on the
  road,
Scarce noticed 'neath a conqueror's
  chariot-wheels.
But his heart trembled, for he wisely
  said:
I am unworthy of this perfect feast:
Lo! I bring offerings to each jealous
  god;

Let not one be forgot, not even the least,
If so I may escape the avenging rod:
Of state too prosperous I am afraid.

FLORENCE.

LIKE some fair woman on whose breast
    are hung
Jewels of price, so decked from side to
    side
With towers and domes and palaces, in
    pride
And state she sits the circling hills
    among.
Into her lap the centuries have flung
Their splendid spoils, and art with art
    has vied
To weave her charmèd raiment to abide
And keep her ever beautiful and young.
And those who pass beneath her potent
    sway
She welcomes nobly, and with royal
    mien
Points where her garnered stores of
    treasure lie.

Take of them what you will, she seems
        to say:
Here are no limits, for a queen am I,
Generous in giving as befits a queen.

SHELLEY.

I.

HE sang the Titan's woes and victory,
Himself a Titan through whose giant
   mind
Astounding shapes swept swifter than
   the wind,
And than the wind more grand and high
   and free.
Ever his ardent vision seemed to see
Amid the glorious structures he de-
   signed
Of poetry, the weal of human·kind,
A reign of hope and love and liberty.
Stilled is that heart, so loyal and so
   brave,
Within the compass of a funeral urn,
Beneath the shade of cypresses and
   pines.
But sweet as violets blooming on the
   grave

His voice remains, and bright his proud
    verse shines
As in the skies the deathless planets
    burn.

II.

COR CORDIUM.

ALL that the water and the fire have
    spared,
The purifying elements that blend
With the remembrance of thy early end
Whom the gods loved, now with the
    earth is shared.
Amid a scene of beauty unimpaired
By blot or stain, upon thy grave descend
The cypress shadows while above extend
Such realms of splendor as thy verse
    declared.
O Heart of Hearts ! repose beneath the
    sod.
The immortal spirit marvellously great
Has found on heights of fame its glorious
    seat.
With flaming wings and garments of a
    god,

Upon those mountain-peaks it keeps its
    state
While Time rolls up our plaudits to its
    feet.

ROME, 1881.

ROME AFTER 1870.

MOTHER of Nations, on whose classic
    brow
Glittered in turn the imperial diadem,
The royal fillet, and that brighter gem
With which free men their chosen chief
    endow ;
To-day's fresh crown prints nobler fur-
    rows now
Upon thy front than left by all of them.
New pearls of promise deck thy gar-
    ment's hem,
And thy pulse quivers at a people's vow.
Child of these later times ! yield to thy
    land
Again the blessings it has rendered
    thee !
Last, precious conquest of a valiant
    band,
Weary of bondage, struggling to be
    free,

Resolved on union, — be the strong
　　right Hand
As still thou art the Heart of Italy!

TO ROME.

A GARDEN of Armida wherein flows
A stream of sweet oblivion, where the
    roar
And din of far-off fights is heard no
    more,
Where for all wounds some healing bal-
    sam grows ;
A dream in which no dread of waking
    throws
Its darkling shadow o'er the fancy's
    store,
But where the radiant-fingered hours
    outpour
Long draughts of rest, refreshment, and
    repose ;
Both these, — a vision, an enchanted
    space, —
City of cities ! when the eyes have seen

Thy deeper mysteries, dost thou appear.
Fain would the heart, in homage to thy
grace
And grandeur, cry that the wide world
might hear :
Hail ! mighty Rome ! my mistress and
my queen !

II.

Like an o'erwhelming wind that sweeps
along
The path on which glad bands of pil-
grims come,
Lashing their limbs till they grow stiff
and numb,
Smiting their lips and robbing them of
song ;
So do thy mighty shadows move among
The daily shows, upon their fronts the
sum
And story of the Past ; and speech is
dumb,
And dead desire before that wondrous
throng.
What should he prate whose ear is
strained to catch

Their voiceless accents? how torment
    the heart
With thoughts aside from their imperi-
    ous sway?
Back, every crowding image, while we
    watch
The spirits' progress, and e'en thou de-
    part,
O Love! unanswered; this is not thy
    day.

III.

As in the presence of the loved one fly,
For him who loves, the golden-wingèd
    hours,
So 'mid the circle of thy charm, with
    showers
Of gifts and benisons the days go by.
And as his mistress still the lover's eye
Invests with new-found beauties, so
    fresh flowers
Upon thy bounteous lap the lavish Pow-
    ers
Seem to our dazzled sight to multiply.
And one divinely-drunken spirit nods

Above the cup thou bear'st, crying:
    'T is fraught
With joy; drink deep while the wine
    overflows.
But one more wise a warning word be-
    stows ;
Heart! let thy bliss be tempered by the
    thought —
Excess of rapture pleases not the gods.

ANTINOUS OF THE VATICAN.

ANTINOUS, upon thy brow of snow
It seems as if the gathered sunshine lay
Of ages, and about thy sweet lips play
The same glad smiles that wreathed
    them long ago.
Thy curls' luxuriant clusters seem to
    glow
With the old life ; we almost hear thee
    say
The word thou usedst to murmur in
    that day
When love's kiss burned on thy mouth's
    perfect bow.
O sweetest youth that ever human eyes
Have gazed upon, thou mak'st the heart
    grow warm
Of him who lifts his glance to thee
    above.
And thine, besides the charm of face
    and form,

His higher fame of whom the poet
    cries:
"How noble is his end who dies for
    love!"[1]

[1] "Che bel fin fa chi ben amando more!"

PETRARCH.

A BAS-RELIEF.

A WHITE-ROBED priestess by an altar
    stands,
Whence breath of flowers and flame of
    sacrifice
With intermingled smoke of incense
    rise,
Serving the god with fair and stainless
    hands.
Up an ascending pathway come the
    bands
Of worshippers with gifts; their yearn-
    ing eyes
Turned towards the goal that in the dis-
    tance lies
Like some cloud structure reared in sun-
    set lands.
But now the shrine is reached; each one
    has bowed
Before the gracious presence; each has
    passed,

Leaving his offering, of the adoring
  throng.
Garlands and jewels there are strewn ;
  and last
A smiling youth, bright-haired and eager-
  browed,
Lays at the altar's foot a wreath of song.

ADDIO A ROMA.

SERBA, o città! un silenzio maestoso;
Tu di chi parte non senti il dolore;
Tu sei eterna, e in immortal splendore
Brilla il volto tuo, alto e luminoso,
Verso di te lo sguardo lacrimoso
Volge nell' ultima ora il viaggiatore,
E col pianto misto, dal triste cuore
Prorompe il suo discorso amoroso.
Cara e beata! ti cinge il pensier mio,
Come le braccia nell' ardente amplesso
D' amor l' oggetto stringon del desio.
Tu che mi porti d' ogni mal l' obblio,
E il mio cammin rischiari col riflesso
D' un indicibil gioia — addio, addio!

ON LEAVING ITALY.

As one who gazes on a dear dead face,
When all is o'er, and cannot let it go,
But with hot tears, and accents weak
    with woe,
Pleads for one last reprieve, one little
    space,
Before the grave shall cover all that
    grace
Which even in death the pallid features
    show,
Knowing that while the stream of life
    shall flow,
No newer love this old one can replace ;
So do I turn once more, and yet once
    more,
Land of my love, my lingering look on
    thee.
A month, — a week, — a day ; — it may
    not be :

So sounds the message that the further
     shore
Cries to its messenger th' unfeeling sea.
Farewell, O Italy! my Italy!